Frog and Friends

Frog's Lucky Day

Written by Eve Bunting
Illustrated by Josée Masse

Dear Parents,

All children learn to read at their own pace and in their own way. Some children dive in successfully while others seem to struggle. Regardless of your child's stage of development, this book can be shared together. Although *Frog and Friends* is designed to be a beginning chapter book for newly independent readers, any child can enjoy the stories inside.

Independent Readers: These children can pick up this book and read, comprehend, and get pleasure from it independently. Allow your child to read the book alone. After you have also read the book, discuss the stories together. Discover which parts your child liked best, and share what you enjoyed. Compare the stories to another book or to a real-life occurrence.

Newly Independent Readers: These children are very excited to be reading their "first chapter book." If your child is at this stage, begin by introducing the characters and concepts in the stories. Following your introduction, listen to your child read the book aloud, and offer assistance when needed. Allow your child to look at the pictures to enhance the stories and aid in comprehension. Although this book is considered to be a beginning chapter book, it is really a collection of stories. If your child does not have the endurance to read the entire book, just one of the two stories can be read in a sitting.

Nonreaders and Emergent Readers: These children are not yet ready to tackle the length and depth of this book alone. Instead, read the stories to your child. As you read, ask your child to predict what will happen next. Discuss the plot, characters, and pictures, and talk about what your child likes about each story. Enjoy reading together!

Visit www.I-Am-A-Reader.com for beginning-reader strategies and tips to help your child learn to read.

Joy L. Towner
Professor of Education
Judson University, Elgin, IL

See other books in our I Am A Reader! series

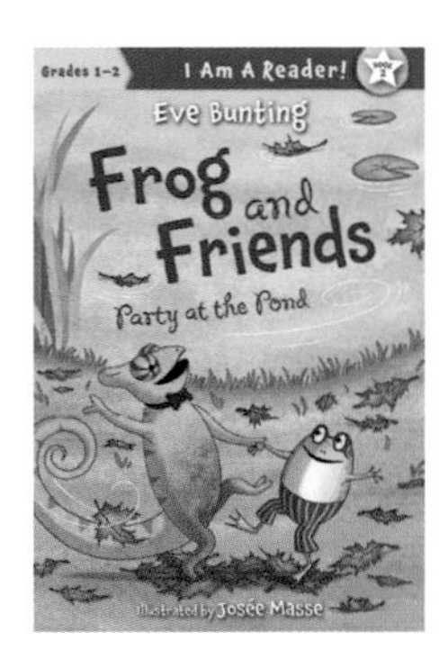

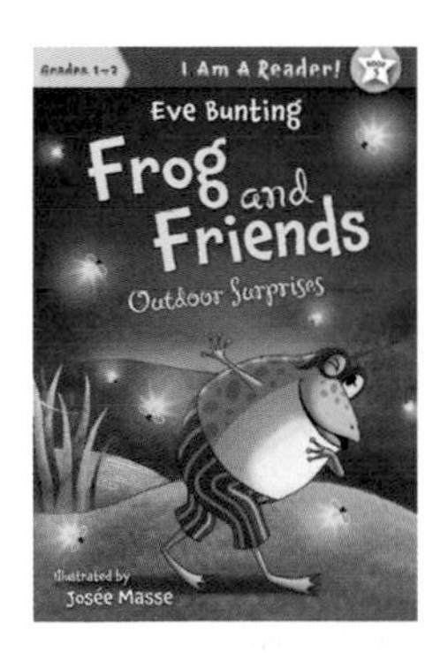

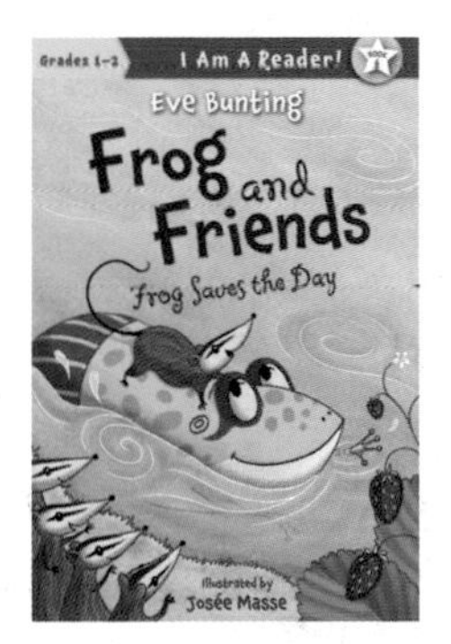

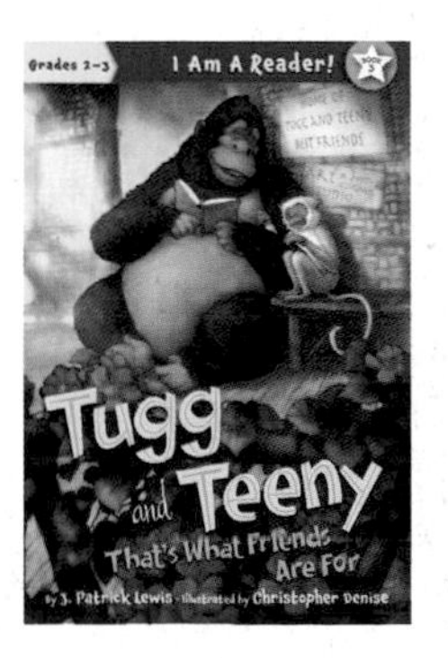

For Shane Davison Bunting, my READER.

—*Eve*

For my dear friends, Guylaine and Marie-Andrée.

—*Josée*

Sleeping Bear Press™
315 E. Eisenhower Parkway, Ste. 200
Ann Arbor, MI 48108
www.sleepingbearpress.com

Printed and bound in the United States.

10 9 8 7 6 5 4 3 2 1 (case)
10 9 8 7 6 5 4 3 2 1 (pbk)

Library of Congress Cataloging-in-Publication Data • Bunting, Eve, 1928- • Frog and friends : Frog's lucky day / written by Eve Bunting ; • illustrated by Josee Masse. • pages cm – (I am a reader! ; bk. 7) • Summary: "A beginning reader book containing two stories in which Frog and his friends try to find the end of the rainbow and Frog looks for a new pond when an unwelcome visitor won't leave his"–Provided by publisher. • ISBN 978-1-58536-892-1 (hard cover) – ISBN 978-1-58536-893-8 (paper back) • [1. Frogs–Fiction. 2. Animals–Fiction. 3. Friendship–Fiction. 4. Ponds–Fiction.] I. Masse, Josée, illustrator. II. Title. III. Title: Frog's lucky day. • PZ7.B91527Fsh 2014 • [E]–dc23 • 2013029265

Table of Contents

I See a Rainbow

"Look!" Frog pointed up. "I see a rainbow."

Possum and Raccoon and Rabbit and Squirrel and Chameleon and little Jumping Mouse looked at the sky.

The little possums jumped up and down. **"Look! Look! Look!"** they shouted.

"Oh, the rainbow is so lovely," Possum said.

“It is all colors,” she told Chameleon. “Like you.”

Chameleon blushed. Today he was green.

“It is much prettier than I am,” he said.

“That is not true,” Frog said. “You are very pretty.”

Everyone sat around the pond counting colors on the rainbow. One, two, three, four, five, six, seven.

"Red, orange, yellow, green, blue, indigo, and violet," Jumping Mouse chanted.

“There is a magic story about a rainbow,” she said.

Jumping Mouse knew a lot because she liked to play in people’s houses.

She liked to listen when they talked.

"There is a pot of gold at the end of a rainbow," she told them. "But no one has ever found the place where the rainbow ends."

"Why not?" Squirrel asked.

"It is hard to find," little Jumping Mouse said.

Squirrel ran up a tall, tall tree.

"I see the end of it!" he shouted. "The end is in that field-that-nobody-owns. We could go there and find the gold."

“We do not need gold,” Chameleon said.

Frog smiled. “No. But it would be nice to be the first to find the end of a rainbow.”

“Good! Good! Good!” the little possums shouted.

They loved to go on field trips.

Frog and his friends walked across grass.

Under trees.

Around rocks.

They were all tired when they got to the field-that-nobody-owned.

Rabbit scratched her head.

"I do not see the end of the rainbow," she said.

"I think it is behind that gray cloud," Frog said. "But this must be the end of the rainbow. Look at all the gold!"

Everyone gasped!

Frog was so excited he hopped too high and fell over.

Raccoon helped him up.

Squirrel clapped his paws. "So much! All over the field-that-nobody-owns."

"Too much to put in one pot," Possum added.

Her little possums jumped off her tail and ran through the field.

"It is not the kind of gold we thought," Chameleon said. "It is better."

Frog smiled. "Yes! Yes! Yes!" he said. "Golden dandelions! What could be nicer?"

"Shall we take some back with us?" Rabbit asked.

Frog shook his head.

"Someone else may be looking for the end of the rainbow. We will leave it for the someone else to find and enjoy."

"We found it first. That is what we wanted," Rabbit said.

"Who will know that we found it first?" Raccoon asked.

"*We* will," Frog said. "That is what is important."

He was happy.

But also tired.

He knew that tonight he would sleep well.

And dream of rainbows.

No Fishing

Frog watched the fisherman walking toward the pond.

He was carrying a folding chair. And a box. And a fishing pole.

Oh no! Frog thought.

I wish I could tell him there are no fish in my pond. He will find out.

The fisherman dropped a hook and line into the water.

The hook had bait on its point.

Frog dived deep.

But the hook trailed this way and that way in the pond.

Frog had to jump over it.

He had to slide under it.

Or swim around it.

"Help! Help!" Frog croaked.

Raccoon came.

She stood near the pond and made a scary face.

The fisherman did not see her.

Squirrel came and threw acorns at him.

The fisherman did not move.

Possum brought her little possums.

"There are no fish in this pond," the little possums shouted. "Go away!"

The fisherman did not hear.

He fished all day.

By nighttime Frog was very tired.

He'd been jumping and sliding, and swimming and hiding all day long.

Rabbit came.

"Oh dear! You are shaking."

She stroked Frog's head.

“I am afraid the fisherman will come back,” Frog said. “He does not care that there are no fish. He likes it here. I must leave my pond and go someplace else.”

“Oh no!” his friends cried. “No! Please. Don’t move! How can we do without you?”

“I have to go,” Frog said. “I am worn out.”

They huddled together and cried.

Then they dried their eyes.

Little Jumping Mouse blew her nose.

"We know you are in danger," she said.

Chameleon turned pale with sorrow.

"What has to be has to be," Raccoon told him.

She helped Frog tie on his pretty blue scarf.

"I will miss you all so much," Frog said.

"We will walk with you," Rabbit told him.

They walked slowly.

As they walked they sang a sad song.

Little Jumping Mouse held Frog's hand.

After a while they came to another pond.

It had a sign beside it that said **NO FISHING.**

"I will be safe here," Frog said. "I will try to be happy."

It was a nice pond.

But it was not his home.

He tried not to show his friends how unhappy he was.

Then he saw a big trash can.

In the can was another **NO FISHING** sign.

An old one.

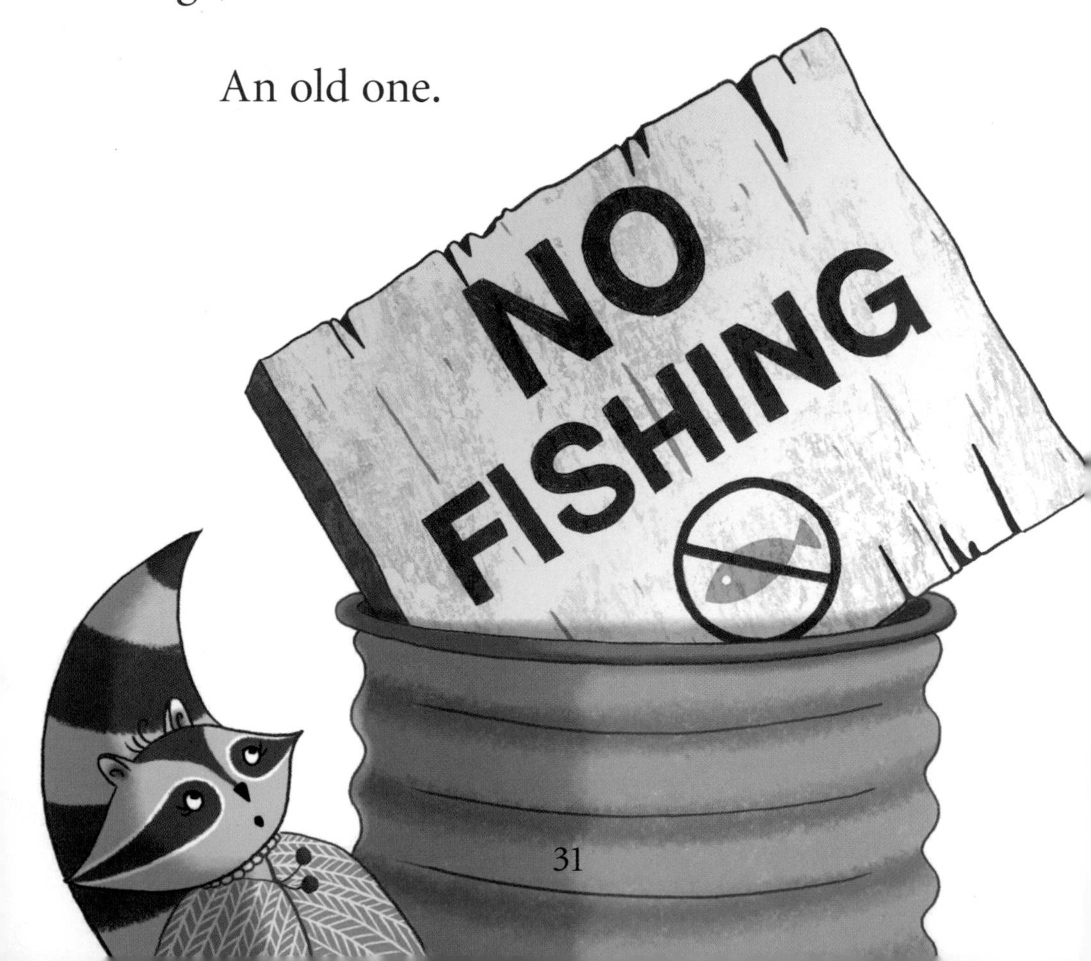

“Oh,” Frog said. “They got a new sign. They threw this one away. We will take it.”

He smiled his biggest smile.

“I will not move to *this* pond,” he said. “This sign will move to *my* pond.”

"Great idea! Hurrah! Hurrah!" his friends shouted.

Together they pulled the sign from the trash can.

Together they carried it back to Frog's pond.

NO FISHING the sign said in big, big letters.

"Welcome to my pond," Frog told it.

He felt better already.